Georgie's Christmas Carol

Other books by Robert Bright

GEORGIE

GEORGIE AND THE BABY BIRDS

GEORGIE AND THE BALL OF YARN

GEORGIE AND THE BURIED TREASURE

GEORGIE AND THE LITTLE DOG

GEORGIE AND THE MAGICIAN

GEORGIE AND THE NOISY GHOST

GEORGIE AND THE ROBBERS

GEORGIE AND THE RUNAWAY BALLOON

GEORGIE GOES WEST

GEORGIE TO THE RESCUE

GEORGIE'S HALLOWEEN

ME & THE BEARS

Georgie's Christmas Carol

by Robert Bright

A TRUMPET CLUB SPECIAL EDITION

Published by The Trumpet Club
666 Fifth Avenue, New York, New York 10103

ISBN: 0-440-84311-1

This edition published by arrangement with Doubleday,
a division of Bantam Doubleday Dell Publishing Group, Inc.
Printed in the United States of America
November 1990

10 9 8 7 6 5 4 3 2 1
UPC

For Sara

Georgie's Christmas Carol

Christmas was coming and Georgie, the little ghost, and Herman the cat were in Mr. Whittaker's workshop watching him make toys and fix up old ones like new. He was enjoying himself so much he was about to forget to do his chores again.

As for Mrs. Whittaker, she was so busy knitting presents in the
parlor, she kept forgetting it was time for bed. Georgie had to
come down from his attic and creak the stairs and squeak the
parlor door extra loud to remind her.

Meanwhile everybody helped to decorate the big tree that grew on the Village Green. Miss Oliver the owl perched on top of the tree and had the best view of all the fun.

And that's the way it was every year. Everybody was getting ready for Christmas and everybody was getting merrier and merrier.

That is everybody except Mr. Gloams who lived in the big house on the hill. He got gloomier and gloomier. Nobody knew why or cared to ask. Because Mr. Gloams was so crotchety he'd never tell. But this year there was a surprise, and it was a lucky thing Georgie found out about it.

What happened was that two unexpected visitors—Sara and Tony—arrived from another town. They were the children of Mr. Gloams's own young sister. But she was being called away over Christmas. So would Mr. Gloams look after them? She was sure he wouldn't mind..

But he did mind. First thing he locked the doors so Sara and Tony couldn't get out and bring germs into the house. And he told them not to expect anything from him for Christmas. Because in his house Christmas was just like any other day—only worse.

Sara and Tony could see that here was a very unhappy man who needed cheering up. So they told him not to worry because Santa Claus would come and take care of everything. And just to make sure they would write him a letter.

At that, Mr. Gloams shook his stick at them. "Santa Claus!" he growled. "I'll tell you about him! Once when I was a little boy I wrote a letter to Santa Claus. I asked him for a sled—just a little sled. But did he bring me that sled? NO! Did anybody ever give me a sled? NO!! So I learned my lesson. You never get anything you don't get for yourself. And that's why I live in a fine big house today." But Sara and Tony couldn't see the sense of living in a fine big house if all it did was to make you gloomy.

So they wrote the letter anyway. Tony did the writing because he spelled better, but Sara told him what to say. And that was a good letter. But who was going to mail it? Mr. Gloams wouldn't and nobody else ever came near that gloomy house. But they *had* to give it to somebody!

So late one afternoon, while Mr. Gloams was taking a nap, Tony and Sara sneaked out of a back window. They made a cheerful little snowman, and gave *him* the letter. They felt sure Santa Claus would see it Christmas Night when he came with his reindeer. But there was a nice cow who saw it first.

16

Now that nice cow happened to be the harmless cow who lived in the barn. She went right down to the Whittakers' house and told Georgie and Herman and Miss Oliver that there were children staying at the Gloams's place and that they had built a snowman and given him a letter.

So they all went up there and Georgie read the letter out loud.
This is what it said:

Dear Santa,

We are at Mr. Gloams' big house. But Mr. Gloams is very gloomy because nobody ever gave him a sled for Christmas when he was a little boy. So please, dear Santa, will you bring Mr. Gloams a sled for Christmas so he wont be gloomy any more and be HAPPY. And can you bring my sister Sara a little doll and me a little toy train. But dont forget the sled. PLEASE.

Tony

19

Now a proper attic has everything in it you ever heard of. But you have to rummage around a lot. Georgie and Herman turned the Whittaker attic upside down. And they found a doll and a train and a sled. But they all needed fixing.

So they put the doll in the parlor. And Mrs. Whittaker no
sooner set eyes on it than she began to knit and sew that doll
a whole fresh outfit.

And they put the train and sled in the workshop. And Mr.
Whittaker took one look and began to fix that train and that
sled as good as new. But he had to work late into Christmas
Night to get them done on time.

As soon as Mr. and Mrs. Whittaker were in bed and asleep
Georgie and his friends took everything to the cowbarn and
closed the doors behind them. Because this was all to be very
secret.

Now up on the hill Mr. Gloams went
to sleep with earmuffs on to keep
out cheerful noises.

But that made it easy for Sara and Tony to sneak one of his stockings. Then they got their own two and ran downstairs.

They hung three stockings on the mantelpiece.

Now it was late and Sara and Tony were sleepy. But they stood in the window and waited for Santa Claus. Because they knew somebody had taken the letter, and they were sure Santa Claus was coming. And so he did. They saw him with their own eyes.

They saw a cat with a bell and an owl with a wreath, and a big fat reindeer pulling a sled with presents. And they saw a very little Santa Claus with a little tree. "What a handy Santa Claus to come down the chimney!" they thought, and ran to the fireplace to wait for him.

But by the time Georgie had gotten the
presents on the roof and squeezed himself
into the chimney,

and slid downstairs, Sara and Tony were fast asleep.

Georgie had to make
several trips and he
even got a little sooty.

32

But the sled was too big for the chimney and had to be left on the stoop. Then the cow went home to her barn, and Georgie and Herman and Miss Oliver went home to the Whittakers. But they'd all be back in the morning to see what happened.

33

Next morning Mr. Gloams came down
earlier than anybody else all dressed for
a gloomy walk. But when he saw what he
saw, he couldn't believe it and made
straight for the door.

There was a sled. And it had his own name on it.

But he was so sure it was a trick that he took the sled and dumped it in the snow. And that would have been the end of it, except he was so fussed up by now

he had to sit down. And that's
when he felt somebody give him
something that felt just like
a push.

Next thing Mr. Gloams knew, he was sliding down the hill on
that sled, and he couldn't believe what was happening to him.
He slid right past the cowbarn

and past Mr. and Mrs.
Whittaker, riding in
a sleigh.

And down the long road into the village.

That sled slid so fast and so far, it slid all the way to the tree on the Green. And everybody shouted:
"MERRY CHRISTMAS, MR. GLOAMS!"

And Mr. Gloams shouted right back: "A
VERY MERRY CHRISTMAS TO YOU!"
And then he knew what was happening to
him. He wasn't *gloomy* any more.

43

He was *merry*

just like everybody else.

44

Thank goodness!

45

Robert Bright was born on Cape Cod, spent his childhood in Europe, and completed his education at Phillips Academy, Andover, and Princeton University.

After becoming a successful advertising executive, Mr. Bright decided he'd had enough of the New York business world, and so, in 1936, he packed up his family and moved to Taos, New Mexico, to begin a new career as a writer. Since then he has been a distinguished newspaper reporter, art and music critic, teacher, novelist, and author/illustrator of more than two dozen books for children. Georgie, the friendly little ghost, first appeared in 1944 and has been charming young readers on both sides of the Atlantic ever since.

A resident of San Francisco, Robert Bright finds the happy inspiration for his Georgie books—initially furnished by his children, Beatrice and Robin—now provided by his grandchildren, Michael, Christopher, Sara, and Tony.